Lila's Harbor

written by CJ Talbert
illustrated by Meg Sodano

.d
soul of Stewart Park's Playground
Campaign, uniting us behind a vision
of an accessible playground where
ALL children could play side by side.

Elayne loved learning, children and
books and was instrumental in
building the Tompkins County Public
Library.

She was a sister, wife, mother,
grandmother, and dear friend. We
miss her good humor, warmth and
zeal for life.

Elayne's Lending Library welcomes
you — as Elayne would have— to
dive into a new story.

WE ENCOURAGE YOU TO BRING THIS BOOK HOME TO READ
THEN RETURN IT SO OTHERS MAY ENJOY IT,
OR PASS IT ALONG TO A FRIEND.

Friends of
STEWART PARK

Learn about the Elayne's Lending Library &
other Stewart Park revitalization projects at
www.stewartpark.org

Lila's Harbor

Text copyright © 2017 by CJ Talbert

Illustrations copyright © 2017 by Meg Sodano

Published by CJT Publishing

Book design by Meg Sodano
The illustrations were rendered with pencil, watersouble crayons, and digital techniques. MSodanoIllustration.com

ISBN 978-0-692-83362-9

*For my beautiful and
inspiring daughter, Lila*

Into town and 'round the bend,
the harbor's full of fishermen.

At the crab traps, we meet Ben.
In his basket, he has ten.

We walk past the fishing lines
with the smell of fish and brine.
Cleaning up his gear is Klein.
Count his rods and reels to nine.

Down the dock, we spot a mate
organizing lures and bait.
We say, "Hello," and so does Kate.
In her tackle, count to eight.

Boats with motors stop their revvin',
find their slips, and gently head in.
Throwing line to port is Kevin.
Tying knots, we count to seven.

Skipping 'cross the planks and sticks,
jolly as we get our kicks,
past a barge we know is Rick's,
see the hoist with pulleys – six.

Display the flags as they arrive,
Catch of the Day and *We Sell Live!*

"Get 'em here and fresh!" says Clive.
In his tank, we count to five.

Rowing boats with colored oars,
dinghies land upon the shore,
dropping anchors just like Thor.
Underwater, we see four.

One with nature is the key.
Sleeping on the deck, we see,
snoozing in a hammock, Lee.
Seagulls perched upon him – three.

In the shallows, we then view,
fishing in her waders blue,
casting out her line is Sue.
Bobbers bobbing, we spot two.

The harbor's beauty, sea, and sun –
with lots to see, we're having fun!

At dock's end, we meet with Juan.
In his hand, his catch of one.

As we look upon the sea
and all our friends we got to see,
wave your hand and smile with me.
Counting down from ten are we.